I0621608

Release Your Thoughts

Use this free write space to let your ink do the talking. This is a no judgement zone for you to release your thoughts without fear of who may or may not like it. Flush out your feelings, and take moments in silence to become better acquainted with the unique soul that you are.

Created by Bleeding Ink Creatives, LLC for the creative mind that loves to write it all out.

Bleeding Ink, A Creative's Haven

Available for sale exclusively via
www.bleedinginkcreatives.com

Bleeding Ink, A Creative's Haven

Write Your Heart Out

Write Your Heart Out

Bleeding Ink, A Creative's Haven

Write Your Heart Out

Bleeding Ink, A Creative's Haven

Write Your Heart Out

Write Your Heart Out

Bleeding Ink, A Creative's Haven

Write Your Heart Out

Write Your Heart Out

Write Your Heart Out

Write Your Heart Out

Bleeding Ink, A Creative's Haven

Write Your Heart Out

Write Your Heart Out

Bleeding Ink, A Creative's Haven

Write Your Heart Out

Write Your Heart Out

Bleeding Ink, A Creative's Haven

Write Your Heart Out

Write Your Heart Out

Bleeding Ink, A Creative's Haven

Write Your Heart Out

Write Your Heart Out

Write Your Heart Out

Write Your Heart Out

Write Your Heart Out

Bleeding Ink, A Creative's Haven

Write Your Heart Out

Write Your Heart Out

Write Your Heart Out

Write Your Heart Out

Write Your Heart Out

Bleeding Ink, A Creative's Haven

Write Your Heart Out

Write Your Heart Out

Write Your Heart Out

Write Your Heart Out

Write Your Heart Out

Bleeding Ink, A Creative's Haven

Write Your Heart Out

Write Your Heart Out

Write Your Heart Out

Write Your Heart Out

Write Your Heart Out

Write Your Heart Out

Write Your Heart Out

Write Your Heart Out

Write Your Heart Out

Write Your Heart Out

Bleeding Ink, A Creative's Haven

Write Your Heart Out

Write Your Heart Out

Write Your Heart Out

Write Your Heart Out

Write Your Heart Out

Write Your Heart Out

Write Your Heart Out

Write Your Heart Out

Write Your Heart Out

Write Your Heart Out

Write Your Heart Out

Write Your Heart Out

Write Your Heart Out

Write Your Heart Out

Write Your Heart Out

Write Your Heart Out

Write Your Heart Out

Write Your Heart Out

Write Your Heart Out

Write Your Heart Out

Write Your Heart Out

Write Your Heart Out

Write Your Heart Out

Bleeding Ink, A Creative's Haven

Write Your Heart Out

Write Your Heart Out

Write Your Heart Out

Write Your Heart Out

Bleeding Ink, A Creative's Haven

Write Your Heart Out

Write Your Heart Out

Write Your Heart Out

Write Your Heart Out

Bleeding Ink, A Creative's Haven

Write Your Heart Out

Write Your Heart Out

Write Your Heart Out

Write Your Heart Out

Write Your Heart Out

Write Your Heart Out

Write Your Heart Out

Write Your Heart Out

Write Your Heart Out

Write Your Heart Out

Write Your Heart Out

Write Your Heart Out

Write Your Heart Out

Bleeding Ink, A Creative's Haven

Write Your Heart Out

Write Your Heart Out

Write Your Heart Out

Write Your Heart Out

Write Your Heart Out

Write Your Heart Out

Write Your Heart Out

Write Your Heart Out

Bleeding Ink, A Creative's Haven

Write Your Heart Out

Write Your Heart Out

Write Your Heart Out

Write Your Heart Out

Write Your Heart Out

Write Your Heart Out

Write Your Heart Out

Write Your Heart Out

Write Your Heart Out

Write Your Heart Out

Write Your Heart Out

Write Your Heart Out

Write Your Heart Out

Write Your Heart Out

Write Your Heart Out

Write Your Heart Out

Write Your Heart Out

Write Your Heart Out

Write Your Heart Out

Write Your Heart Out

Write Your Heart Out

Write Your Heart Out

Write Your Heart Out

Write Your Heart Out

Write Your Heart Out

Write Your Heart Out

Write Your Heart Out

Write Your Heart Out

Write Your Heart Out

Write Your Heart Out

Write Your Heart Out

Write Your Heart Out

Write Your Heart Out

Write Your Heart Out

Write Your Heart Out

Write Your Heart Out

Bleeding Ink, A Creative's Haven

Write Your Heart Out

Write Your Heart Out

Write Your Heart Out

Write Your Heart Out

Write Your Heart Out

Write Your Heart Out

Write Your Heart Out

Write Your Heart Out

Write Your Heart Out

Bleeding Ink, A Creative's Haven

Write Your Heart Out

Write Your Heart Out

Bleeding Ink, A Creative's Haven

Write Your Heart Out

Bleeding Ink, A Creative's Haven